THE WENDIGO INCIDENT

AN OLD WORLD SAGA NOVELETTE

THE WENDIGO INCIDENT: AN OLD WORLD SAGA NOVELETTE

First edition published July 2021

Book cover art by warrendesign.
Manuscript design by Joel Preston.
Graphics included in manuscript from Adobe Stock, original design by SeemaLotion. Further graphics sourced from Freepik.com

ISBN: 978-0-6452489-0-6 (E-Book)
ISBN: 978-0-6452489-1-3 (Paperback)

To contact the author email: contact@joelprestonauthor.com
joelprestonauthor.com

THE WENDIGO INCIDENT

AN OLD WORLD SAGA NOVELETTE

JOEL PRESTON

Other Novels by This Author:

In the Shadow of Monstrous Things

Rise Golden Apollo

In the Shadow of The Old World

Fall Silver Artemis

Novellas by This Author:

Fear the Full Moon: An Old World Saga Novella

Earth's Mightiest Warrior: An Old World Saga Novella

Strange Lights in a Dark World: An Old World Saga Novella

This novelette is dedicated Elizabeth King, Alexandra Marshall and Michael Fomiatti, whose help and support have allowed The Old World Saga to come this far.

IN READING ORDER

This novella takes place **between** *The Old World Saga Book Two*: **Rise Golden Apollo** and *The Old World Saga Book Three*: **In the Shadow of The Old World.**

For maximum enjoyment of this novelette it is best to have read the preceding books before beginning. Fear the Full Moon should be read before this novelette.

1.  IN THE SHADOW OF MONSTROUS THINGS

2.  RISE GOLDEN APOLLO

3.  FEAR THE FULL MOON

4.  THE WENDIGO INCIDENT

5.  IN THE SHADOW OF THE OLD WORLD

6.  EARTH'S MIGHTIEST WARRIOR

7.  FALL SILVER ARTEMIS

8.  STRANGE LIGHTS IN A DARK WORLD

9. IN THE SHADOW OF THE SUNDERED KING

(coming soon)

CHAPTER ONE

ENDLESS HUNGER

Amber yawned and stretched her arms out of her claustrophobic coffin of a sleeping bag.

She hadn't been asleep for long and could still hear the crackling of the fire outside. Its glow pierced the sides of her green canvas tent.

Through the hatch in the roof she saw the twinkling stars in the clear sky above. Away from the lights of the city they were exceptionally bright. However, their beauty quickly dulled as feeling returned to Amber's body.

The throbbing in her head indicated that she'd had too much of a good time. Now, desperately dehydrated and needing to answer the call of nature, she shuffled from her sleeping bag and fumbled for the closed zip of the tent.

Amber was nineteen years old and in her first year at university in Minneapolis. She had been popular in high school, and that translated well into college life. She was smart enough to know that she skated through life on her looks. A wink at the teacher or a giggle towards the professor and any grade could be fixed. She was blessed with traditional American beauty, the type you see from cheerleaders in movies. She had often considered moving away from that kind of shallow, vacant life after high school. But it turned out she loved the attention and adoration. The likes on social media and the unending messages filled her with a hollow love that she ate up.

Amber had to embrace her true self. She made friends with some senior frat boys and their socialite girlfriends. Popularity, status and all of their associated perks were hers to enjoy.

When the boys had suggested a camping trip over the weekend, Amber just couldn't say no.

They'd partied well into the early hours of the morning. By the sounds of it, everyone had now retired or passed out. Other than the dying fire, all was quiet.

She paused as she reached for the zip.

There was another sound; she just hadn't picked up on it. It was like a soft ripping or tearing, coming from not too far away.

Brushing her hair over her shoulder, Amber chose to ignore the funny noise and stepped out into the night air.

She looked around their campsite. It was a warzone. Broken bottles lay scattered about the leaf litter and a whole tray of raw sausages had been discarded on the ground. She made a mental note that she should clean that up, lest it attract wild animals.

She giggled to herself as she thought about some of the monster stories the guys had been telling earlier in the evening. Native American burial grounds and lonely cabins sat in the forefront of her mind as she stumbled into the dark.

One of the guys, Kelly, had been muttering that he kept seeing some ghastly shape out of the corner of his eyes. Like there was a malevolent supernatural force moving in the mist. Kelly had always been a jokester.

Kelly's best friend, Sam, had been really egging him on. Amber didn't really like Sam. He was known for bizarre late-night excursions and hanging out with odd people. He spent hours locked away reading, and sometimes, she thought she heard chanting coming from his dorm room. Amber believed that Sam was growing more and more unhinged, but their circle of friends didn't bother to acknowledge it.

The fire sat in the centre of a semi-circle of tents. Sparks burst into the air as a log collapsed into the burning coals.

Amber could see two distinctly human shapes silhouetted against the darkness on the other side of the dying flames. One was crouched and the other was lying down.

"What are you guys doing?" Amber yawned, taking a step towards them.

The crouched figure's head locked onto her and froze. Amber just giggled. The guys must be goofing around. He was like a deer in the headlights, remaining completely still as she approached.

Amber kept walking until she passed the fire. As her eyes adjusted to the night, she could make out who the crouched person was. The burly wide-shouldered outline of Kelly was always recognisable. He was a football player and senior heartthrob.

The person on the ground wasn't moving at all.

As the firelight lessened, Amber felt a sudden spike in anxiety.

There was a splash as her foot landed in a pool of liquid.

Amber looked at the forest floor. It was too dark to see what she'd stepped in, but something made her think the worst.

"Blood?" she thought. *"Surely not..."*

Kelly rose to his feet and turned to face her. His features were still entirely dark, yet radiating from him was a terrifying, foreboding aura.

Amber stepped back. "What's up with you?" she demanded.

She heard his raspy slow breaths. He didn't speak.

Something was definitely wrong. Amber listened to her instincts and turned around.

She ran back towards the fire.

Kelly bolted after her. He lunged awkwardly. It was like he'd lost all sense of his own body.

Amber tripped over a backpack.

Suddenly, Kelly was looming over her. In the orange light, his deformity was revealed.

The once handsome face of the football player was now disfigured. His skin was pale and his eyes were entirely black. Red veins weaved around his eyelids and across his upper cheeks. From his teeth dangled loose tendons. It looked like he'd been eating raw flesh. Blood dripped down his chin and from his hands.

"KELLY, STOP IT!" Amber screamed, hoping her cry would wake her campmates. Through the corner of her eyes, she noticed the other tents flapping open. The others were gone. She was alone.

Kelly turned his head and studied her. His movements were stilted and animalistic. In his blank eyes was a void of cosmic terror.

Amber reached into the fire and grabbed a charred stick. She pointed the flaming end at Kelly and shoved it into his face. Fear and adrenaline didn't let her feel her hand searing and bubbling as she held the improvised weapon.

The demonic Kelly reeled back in anguish and made a blood-curdling noise.

Something in the darkness answered him. It was like a shrill hooting; a sound unlike anything she'd heard before. Amber pushed herself up but quickly felt the firm grip of Kelly's hand wrap around her wrist. She was violently pulled towards her insane friend.

With her free arm, she pushed his face. She aimed for his eyes, but Kelly violently fidgeted. Amber's middle finger slid into Kelly's snarling mouth, and he bit down hard.

Amber screamed as blood burst in a fountain from the spot her finger had been.

Sickening cracks filled the night as Kelly started chewing on the appendage. Amber ran for it.

She took one last look at Kelly's twisted face as she bolted away, but she barely registered him. Moving behind the wisps of smoke from the fire, somewhere in the not-so-distant trees was a giant figure. She only saw it for a second. But that second was enough.

Horror beyond words was lingering in the forest. What Amber saw she could barely comprehend. The shrill hooting followed her into the night.

The darkness of the forest was her only chance of escape. It was either her end or her salvation.

The blank eyes of Kelly watched her leave.

Deep in those woods of northern Minnesota, the lone figure of Amber plunged knee-deep into a pungent invisible bog.

She didn't even feel the putrid water sloshing around her as she pushed on. Her mind raced with horror as images of the night flashed across her eyes. She felt faint; presumably from the steady stream of blood pouring from where her finger had been. The forest was growing dizzier and dizzier the deeper into its depths she traversed.

In the black of the night, she didn't feel alone. It was like there were ever-present eyes following her through the trees. Occasionally, she thought she caught glimpses of the giant figure in the distance, but it was just the illusion of shadows in the lingering mist.

Amber clambered up a muddy bank and onto dry land. The Pine Island State Forest was known for vast swathes of trees surrounded by bogs and marshes. If a person could stick to dry land, it was beautiful.

Now, alone in the dark, the forest was terrifying.

"Amber! Amber! Is that you?" a shrill voice cried.

Amber turned around to see someone with a torch fast approaching.

"Nina!" Amber said woozily. "Thank god you're okay!"

A heavy thumping followed Nina, and soon another of her friends emerged.

"Arj! What happened to you guys?"

Arj was a dark-skinned lanky football player with shoulder-length dreadlocks. Usually, he was all jokes, but now he looked haunted and fearful.

"There is something in the woods," he said, grabbing Amber on the shoulders. "Oh my god! What happened to your finger?"

"It was Kelly, he bit it off," Amber grimaced. "Where is he?"

"I don't know," Arj replied. "Both Kelly and Sam have gone insane."

Arj pulled the shirt from his back and tore a long piece of fabric from it. He wrapped it tightly around Amber's hand, slightly stemming the loss of the blood.

"Kelly was eating Julian!" Nina cried. "I saw him! He was pulling the flesh from his bones like he was a wild dog! Sam was muttering all this crazy stuff and ran off. He said our salvation lay in the cabin, whatever that means."

Amber swallowed her terror and brushed the muck from her face. "I didn't see Sam. We have to find the road," she whispered urgently to Nina and Arj. "You have a light; lead the way."

"But I don't know where to go," Nina sobbed.

"This way, I think," Amber guessed, pointing west.

The two women started forward, but Amber quickly stopped when Arj's thumping footsteps failed to follow.

"What are you-"

"Shh!" Arj urged. He was staring intently into the darkness behind them.

"Do you see it?" Arj muttered.

"No, it's too dark! Arj, come on!" Amber pleaded.

Arj didn't budge. He was transfixed by something in the distant trees.

"Something huge is moving out there…."

"It might be Kelly or Sam, so we have to get out of here."

"No," Arj said sternly. "Too big…"

Arj sounded dreary, almost sleepy.

Amber slapped Arj in the face, and Arj snapped from his trance. He took the torch from Nina and moved to the front of the group.

The three college students bolted through the woods, barrelling through the underbrush and leaping over tree roots. Only the distant howling of wolves could be heard as they crunched their way through the forest.

After fifteen minutes, they paused to catch their breath.

"What happened at camp?" Amber asked.

Arj answered shakily, "We were drinking… then Kelly went all weird…."

"So did Sam!" Nina interjected. "They both said they saw something moving in the forest. A stag. But, like, a giant one."

"Sam kept fidgeting with that green octopus necklace of his. He was saying something about the cold waste and distant drums in the dark," Arj added. "He was acting really weird."

"They both just sort of zoned out, then Kelly attacked Julian."

"I saw something in the forest by camp too," Amber said quietly.

"Yeah, I keep seeing it," Arj said. "Like in the corner of my eyes. Something is following us."

"On the way here, you were talking about curses and myths in this forest. What did you say again?" Amber asked Arj.

"That was all Kelly," Arj muttered. "He said that they're ancestral monsters to the indigenous people of this area that prowl the forest. But, of course, you know how he was…."

A branch cracked near them. Then another. The cold hooting sprang up again.

"We have to go!" Nina urged.

Arj didn't move. He was once again staring into the dark trees.

"Do you see it!" he said excitedly.

"See what?" Amber said, peering into the darkness.

Arj didn't answer. Nina frantically pulled on his shirt.

Again, Arj didn't budge. He was transfixed by something invisible that neither of the others could see.

"Arj!" Amber ordered.

He turned around. Gone were his brown eyes. In their place gleamed malevolent black emptiness.

Arj wrapped his arm around Nina and within moments, his teeth were sinking into her jugular.

Nina looked wide-eyed and surprised as she feebly tried to push him away. Arj withdrew, taking a chunk of Nina's neck with him. He chewed slowly, turning his attention to Amber.

Amber whimpered. Again, she ran.

Across another bog and through another island of tall pines, she leapt, clambered and scurried. She could see an orange glow not more than a hundred yards ahead.

Yes! There was a cabin in a clearing. She could see its tall pointed roof.

The mist was getting thicker around her and the shrill call was growing louder.

The closer Amber got to the cabin, the more panicked the sound became. It was like whatever was making it didn't want to be here.

She swore as she ran.

Salvation was so close, she could make it!

The mist enveloped Amber, and she tripped over a tree root.

She pulled her face from the dirt and looked up.

In the swirling darkness above her, a pair of ghostly white eyes flashed with a deathly glow.

Against the night sky, she saw wide antlers springing from the mist.

Then, Amber's mind turned to other thoughts. She was hungry... so very, very hungry.

The orange lights of the nearby cabin were swallowed by the fog as Amber's eyes turned black.

CHAPTER TWO

RUMOURS FROM ACROSS THE SEA

- JUNE 13 2020 -
THE PENTAGON, WASHINGTON DC

Lieutenant Commander Patrick Leeson steadily marched down one of the long bland halls of the Pentagon. He had the distinct look of a man who'd been called in during his time off, and he wasn't happy about it.

"Sir," a pair of military personnel nodded as he strode past.

Patrick's thoughts were so far away that he barely reacted, only offering a stifled grunt to his colleagues. Sunny California was where he was meant to be right now; sitting on a beach chair, letting the world drift by…

A bald man with a surly expression in a very formal uniform called out to Patrick as he strode past, once again ripping him away from his fantasy.

"Neanderthal! Come here!"

Patrick instantly knew it was him that was being summoned. No one ever called him Patrick the Navy SEAL. He was only known by his infamous call-sign: Neanderthal.

"Commander," Neanderthal said curtly.

"What a surprise it is to see you here in Washington," the man said, slapping Neanderthal on the back.

"I wouldn't be here if I didn't have to be, sir," Neanderthal replied, expressionless.

The senior military man was well-known to everyone in the armed forces. Rolf Bygrave was the Commander of the US Special Operation Command and not a person to cross. He embodied the classic elements of an old-school military manager; namely, if he liked you, you got whatever you wanted. If he didn't like you, your career was as good as dead.

"Man of your esteem shouldn't be cooped up in an office, eh? We could use you and your boys soon," Bygrave stated, saliva hurtling past his bushy moustache. Luckily for Neanderthal, Rolf Bygrave very much liked him.

"What's going on, sir?"

"Not to be talked about in public, I'm afraid," Rolf said, straightening his tunic. "All I can give you is a location: Scandinavia."

Neanderthal raised his eyebrows. He did like the sound of a deployment there.

"Ah good, I see I have your interest. I'll be in touch. Who are you here to see?" Rolf asked.

"Captain Shear," Neanderthal replied. "USSOT business."

Rolf let out a hearty laugh. "USSOT, I'm surprised you waste your time with that garbage."

Neanderthal didn't say anything. He'd always found it best to neither agree nor disagree with the Commander.

"Give Captain Shear my best," Rolf said, rolling his eyes before turning to engage another high-ranking officer in conversation.

Neanderthal walked briskly in the direction of Captain Shear's office.

Rolf Bygrave wasn't the only ranking member of the US military that was dismissive of USSOT. Most thought it was a joke, despite the group's real and very tangible work. Neanderthal supposed that the layers of extreme secrecy didn't help its reputation.

USSOT, or the United States Supernatural Occurrence Taskforce, worked with the unknown. They were sent in to deal with paranormal threats significant enough to warrant an armed response. The group was well-funded but operated strictly within its own command structure.

At the top was Fiona Shear, a stern-faced woman with a distinguished career behind her. She'd spent a lifetime shattering glass ceilings, though she'd never bragged about it. Her sole focus was the job. Rumour had it that Shear had been in Iraq during the initial invasion in 1991 and had spent the best part of the next decade in the Middle East. It was over there that something had happened to get her involved in the paranormal side of the military. Though not even Neanderthal knew what that event had entailed. He had once heard a whisper that Fiona Shear had encountered a 'cosmic entity', whatever that meant.

No matter the hidden truth of the matter, she'd dedicated herself to leading the government response to significant supernatural instances. Instances of such severity that they required a military response were scarce, but from time to time did happen.

Neanderthal had spent a good deal of time in the Middle East during the second invasion. He'd even won an award when his four-man reconnaissance unit fended off a much larger force of anti-coalition militia. They'd been forced into a ravine and had made a final stand. Against fearful odds, Neanderthal had produced a victory that was almost folklore within the military. Since then, he'd had his pick of special missions.

Still, his time in Iraq had transformed the Navy SEAL from a sceptic to a believer. A series of destructive helicopter crashes had befuddled the US military and Neanderthal was one of the soldiers sent to find out what was going on. His team had found odd tribes-people in the desert. Magical tribes-people. And in their command was a bird of monstrous proportions, capable of lifting tanks from the ground.

Neanderthal had won the respect of the bizarre desert-dwelling creatures, allowing the military to take out the bird. Ever since then, Neanderthal had allowed a lot of time for USSOT, and USSOT had always requested him.

The revelation that world was riddled with monsters and magic, despite all of it being a secret, had changed Neanderthal's perspective on things. Despite having blitzed his BUDS training and being renowned as an accomplished soldier, Neanderthal always adopted a stress-free attitude. He didn't overthink things and put conscious effort into approaching every new situation with an open mind. As a result, he was versatile and adaptable. Qualities that the military admired, but that USSOT needed in its operatives.

He reached Captain Shear's office door and knocked.

It opened to reveal the wrinkled, yet dignified, face of Fiona Shear. Beneath her cap, her blonde hair was steadily greying. She had hazel eyes and wore a constant scowl, something that put those who didn't know her on the wrong foot right away. Still, she shook Neanderthal's hand warmly.

"Lieutenant Commander Leeson," she said.

"Ma'am," Neanderthal replied. "You know that you're potentially the only person in the US military who doesn't call me Neanderthal?"

"Call signs are appropriate when in the field, not in the office," Shear stated matter-of-factly, moving towards her desk.

Neanderthal sat down on an unassuming brown chair in front of Shear's desk. Every free corner of the old wooden table was stacked to the brim with poorly bound piles of paper and manilla folders.

"What's the news, ma'am?"

"I have two pieces of information to share with you; and a job."

"You do know that I am currently on rec leave?"

"I am well aware, and don't worry, you will get your time off re-accredited."

"Excellent," Neanderthal nodded. "Thank you."

"Now, down to business," Shear said, pulling the topmost

folder from the haphazardly stacked pile in front of her. "Minnesota, the Pine Island State Forest; we've had an occurrence."

"Something warranting an armed response?"

"Potentially."

She pushed the folder across the desk.

Neanderthal opened it and was confronted by several images of mangled bodies. He pushed them aside and began reading the reports.

"The creature behind the attacks in the forest has been identified."

Neanderthal scanned the pages until he came across a name with paranormal connotations.

"A wendigo," he murmured. "I've done the reading on them."

"Then you will know that they are a rare and formidable creature. Currently, we have no precise knowledge on how to take one down. We assume, like with most monsters of its sort, that silver will do the trick. However, we have a problem."

"The wendigo is mostly an ethereal creature. Difficult to hit with a bullet," Neanderthal pondered out loud.

"Impressive," Shear smiled. "What else can you tell me?"

"The wendigo is known from Native American folklore. It doesn't attack directly. It instead uses its gaze to afflict a lone person with an insatiable appetite for human flesh."

"Yes, the cannibalism monster, I call it. The embodiment of endless hunger."

"But," Neanderthal said slowly, "in the past, it has usually only inflicted its curse upon single people lost deep in remote

woods. That isn't something USSOT is concerned with."

"Normally, no. There are additional circumstances this time. This wendigo has reappeared and has attacked several different groups in the forest. There haven't been any survivors thus far, bar one."

"Multiple attacks in the same spot? Something has riled it up. What did the survivor say? What did it look like?" Neanderthal's curiosity was getting the better of him. By all accounts, the wendigo was one of the most fearsome beings that could appear in North America.

"The survivor's testimony is of little use. You will hear for yourself soon enough. We can only go by previously recorded encounters. The wendigo appears in a wave of mist and is reported to be a giant creature of exposed bone and rotting flesh. It is anthropomorphic with the head of a stag. Yet none who have encountered it and lived have ever gotten a good look because it hides in the fog. On the other hand, there are also the old legends of the wendigo being smaller and more human."

"Multiple forms, perhaps?" Neanderthal offered. "Has the survivor said anything helpful?"

"All he has offered is utter gibberish. The question we want to be answered is why was he let go by the beast."

"Anything unusual about this guy?" Neanderthal asked.

"Yes, he has an FBI file. He's been watched recently for suspected connections to dark cults. Sam Oswald is his name."

Neanderthal found this interesting. A supernatural being let a cultist go... there is no way that was a coincidence.

"What are we talking about here? Cult of Belial?"

"No, something darker, older and far more mysterious. Investigations are still ongoing. But, I suspect the answer lies in those woods. The FBI believe it's the same cult that recently appeared in Florida."

"I'm not familiar with that," Neanderthal stated, lowering the folder.

"A bunch of people, half-naked, dancing around a huge fire deep in the swamp. Police said they were all mad. They said there was something strange… a green idol they were worshipping, unlike anything from our world. They recovered a black stone carved with unknown hieroglyphics. It is all very odd. My liaison said they haven't seen reports like this since the 1920s."

"Has anyone from USSOT directly interviewed the survivor? Perhaps he can shed some light on this cult?"

"No," Shear frowned, crossing her arms. "Our first responders have tried. It appears that this is a case where we need someone afflicted with the supernatural to speak to a victim of the supernatural. Sam's father, Dean, is a prominent business man in Tallahassee, with some suspicious connections of his own. With his son being the only survivor here, it would be foolish to dismiss the possibility of a link between the events in Florida and what has happened in Minnesota. Regardless, you will join the team while we work out just what is going on in those northern woods. I have the utmost faith in you."

"I guess I'm going to Minneapolis then," Neanderthal said, struggling to hide his internal disappointment. The beach seemed like a distant dream now.

"Not right away…." Shear trailed off, once again rummaging

through her piles of papers. "First, you need to take an overseas trip. How does Central Australia sound?"

Neanderthal's jaw dropped. Had he missed something?

Captain Shear continued, "We have intelligence that the Australian Government has a caged monster that could be very helpful in this case. That, and I want some more information about what's going on down there. Funny reports have reached me."

"Hard to escape those rumours," Neanderthal chuckled. "Two werewolves in Australia? I thought, for sure, that was a joke."

"Less a joke and more a deliberate leak of classified information," Shear raised an eyebrow at him.

"Well, I am intrigued," Neanderthal said.

"It is a leak we will use to our advantage, nevertheless," Shear concluded.

"What do you want with the werewolf?" Neanderthal asked, though part of him already suspected the answer.

"What is the best way to kill a monster that is impervious to human methods?" Shear asked.

"Have another supernatural monster do the work for you…" Neanderthal answered.

"Correct. Do the reading I have prepared for you. I suspect that Australia's secret pet may be our best option for removing this monster from the forest, should all else fail."

"Do you think the Australians will release the creature into our custody?"

"Yes, I think so. USSOT has no reason to keep the Australian supernatural department held at arm's length. And I have received a surprising amount of correspondence from their OIC recently. Again, this is just a guess, but I am beginning to suspect there is more going on Down Under than the leak about werewolves suggests."

Neanderthal had to admit that his curiosity was piqued.

"Why me?"

"As this is a diplomatic mission that will involve some… let's say, rigorous negotiation, then I need someone who is up to the job. Since I am stuck here, it falls on you. Pack your bags, Lieutenant Commander Leeson; you will be paying our southern colleagues a surprise visit."

Chapter Three

DOWN UNDER

- JUNE 17 2020 -
LOCATION CLASSIFIED, CENTRAL AUSTRALIA

A tall man stood before a heavy punching bag and breathed in deep. He had long, unkempt brown hair that had started curling at the sides and a thick scraggily beard. If he were anywhere other than the expansive training room, he could've been mistaken for a homeless person about to vent his frustrations.

He punched.

His hand hit the heavy red and black bag with so much force that it swung loose of its chains and collapsed to the floor, spilling sand from the fist-shaped hole now piercing its side.

"You can do better," a bored voice called from behind him.

Joshua Dare ignored the snide remark and resumed his

fighting stance. Today he had the pleasure of being watched by Liam Sager, one of the few permanent members of the Australian Supernatural Taskforce. The AST were an omnipresent part of Josh's life these days.

"You are going to need to buy better punching bags," Josh smirked back at Liam.

Liam shrugged, "It is a pain to get any kind of equipment out here. Control your punches. You can apply enough force to move the bag without breaking it."

"Thanks, sensei," Josh sighed.

Liam was a handsome man with blonde hair and a lean frame. In the short time Josh had known him, Liam had always maintained an immaculately shaved look with a crisp formal haircut. Recently though, he'd been letting his grooming standards slip slightly. His hair was getting longer and fell in an awkward fringe across his face. He also dressed more casually, not strictly adhering to black suits.

"Have you tried the meditation exercises you've been given?" Liam asked.

"Kind of…" Josh murmured. He hated meditating. He simply didn't have the patience for it.

"It was you who originally said you felt the wolf lingering in the back of your mind," Liam interjected impatiently.

"I never said *the wolf*," Josh replied. "It's more like a distant shadow that I can sometimes feel… I dunno, it's hard to explain."

"Well, whether a product of your imagination or not, I want to see how it affects the transformation."

The conversation abruptly ended with the buzzing of Liam's

phone. "Run the course," Liam ordered, before answering the call.

Josh didn't really know how to take Liam as a person. On the one hand he was extremely professional, in the right settings almost coming across as pompous. Yet, he was also, for lack of a better term, a bit of a 'dude-bro'. When he was off work, or surrounded by his friends, he became a much more relaxed, care-free person. In these circumstances he embodied, at least to Josh, what it was to be the typical university-guy.

One thing was for sure though, over the course of the last eight months, something had been eating away at Liam. He was on a mission that Josh wasn't allowed to know about. He'd appear for short stints, before vanishing again to pursue someone, or something, in a remote part of the world. Whatever he was chasing wasn't allowing itself to be caught. Unlike Josh, who by all accounts, had been captured extremely easily.

The padding below Josh's feet stopped a few metres away. It morphed into a gleaming polished floor with a series of obstacles placed across it. It was designed to test speed, reflexes, strength and agility.

Josh moved to the start line and braced. Like a streak of lightning, he took off, weaving around cones and swinging across horizontal bars propped up by steel beams. Damn, was he fit. Josh was nothing like the old version of himself; the ordinary person he'd been before coming here.

The training he was constantly undertaking helped Josh to forget the ever-watchful gaze of the government on him.

He was under constant surveillance. From the outside, he

looked like a perfectly normal twenty-four year old man, albeit a little paler and a lot fitter than the average person at his age.

Joshua Dare was a prisoner. But not an ordinary prisoner.

Josh was being held in a top-secret facility somewhere in Central Australia. The agents that worked in this place called it 'Down Under'. They were underground, though how deep, he wasn't sure. The nearest town was a place called Alice Springs, which was several hours away by car. Josh had never been there.

Josh's story was a ridiculous one.

In mid-2019, Joshua Dare was bitten. Not by a dog or a cat or anything pedestrian like that. He'd fallen victim to the cursed bite of a lycanthrope.

He was a werewolf.

In the months that had followed his first transformation in the northern city of Cairns, death had followed. This was no teenage werewolf fantasy story; his werewolf was a monster to the core. Every full moon Josh transformed into an uncontrollable creature of destruction. The man disappeared in the shadow of the monstrous thing that dwelled inside.

It had all culminated in mid-October when agents of the Vatican had attempted to draw him out by using his friend as bait.

Josh had no idea what had happened to his friends or his girlfriend after that night. No one shared any information with him. He just got told to train.

Despite his incarceration, Josh was treated exceptionally well. The Australian Government staff all had a jovial sense of humour. He was being taught to fight and his strength was being perpetually tested. Often, he passed hours in examination rooms as doctors drew blood and attached electrodes to him. He figured he must've had his brain scanned a hundred times at this point.

The full moon had become a particularly uncomfortable experience. Early in the day, he was sedated. He didn't know what the scientists did to him exactly when that ominous orb rose in its deathly white glory. Josh woke up with no memory the following morning. He was sure it was unpleasant though.

Still, the werewolf curse had yielded some surprising benefits in Josh's day-to-day life. He was lean and muscular, fast and strong. He had a fantastic ability to heal from almost any injury rapidly, though it wasn't an infinite power. Too much damage and his body couldn't handle it.

A secret desire Josh held was control of the beast. He wanted to be able to transform at will and not become a murderous animal. There was so much potential for him to do good with the curse, if only he could control it.

As Josh had learned, the werewolf curse originated in ancient Greece and had steadily mutated over the millennia. Josh was fortunate that he'd received a semi-pure version of the curse and thusly didn't become a skinny, dishevelled creature on the full moon. Instead, his werewolf was tall and coated with long black fur everywhere except for his chest, snout and around his eyes. He'd been shown pictures of himself during the monthly transformation, and he looked cool.

Despite the implied mystery of curses and monsters, Josh's life was becoming rather dull. He didn't have internet. The Australian agents worked on a rotating schedule, so he couldn't even make any friends. The only two that made regular appearances at Down

Under were Liam Sager and the boss, Brett Sayer.

Occasionally, an elderly couple named Jan and Petra came to visit him. Those two didn't enjoy the watchful eyes of the government upon them either. Jan and his wife worked for an organisation called The Old World. That group was a whole different story. It was comprised of supernatural enthusiasts from around the world that studied monsters. While The Old World had the appearance of a rag-tag bunch of eccentric old people, Josh suspected that there was secret money and influential figures at the organisation's heart.

Yet, it had been a month since Jan and Petra had visited. Josh was beginning to feel the loneliness deeper than ever.

Josh picked up the punching bag, spilling further sand to the floor and hooked it back up.

"Joshua," Liam said formally, with his ear still pressed to the phone, "clean yourself up. It appears we have guests."

• • • • •

AFTER TRUDGING BACK to his quarters to shower, Josh threw on a clean white shirt and white slacks. It was bad enough that he was a lab rat; they didn't have to make him dress like one too.

A guard carrying a menacing black rifle collected him and escorted him to a conference room.

Josh struggled to hide his excitement. For the first time in months, something different was happening.

He sat down on a blue office chair and scanned the room.

There were a few people in suits he didn't recognise.

The man at the head of the table was the OIC of the AST, Brett Sayer. He was nearing retirement age with a round face and short black hair. He had thin-framed glasses and still dressed very casually, despite being a senior figure in a secret organisation. His penchant for mountain biking had given him unnervingly muscular legs that he showed off in the shorts he was always wearing.

Today was no different. Brett was dressed in civilian attire and looked annoyed to be there.

Liam entered the room and greeted Brett with a handshake. "Who is here?" he asked.

"Some Navy SEAL arrived in Alice Springs yesterday and has decided to pay us a visit," Brett replied sourly.

"That doesn't sound good," Liam murmured.

"No, it does not."

They didn't have to wait long before there was a knock at the door. Escorted by two Australian Security Intelligence Organisation members, a formally dressed American military man entered the room. His entourage of other US personnel stayed by the door outside.

His gold-buttoned, navy blue jacket's left breast was adorned with ribbons of all colours. He appeared quite young, perhaps late twenties or early thirties, with a square jaw and a clean-shaven face. His neat, medium-length sideburns crawling from beneath his ceremonial cap revealed his brown hair.

Brett got up and shook hands with the newcomer.

"Mr Leeson."

"Mr Sayer," the American replied. His accent was not at all pronounced.

"I am somewhat surprised to see you at Down Under," Sayer frowned, sitting down. He seemed tense.

"Well, I was visiting Pine Gap and thought I'd make the additional journey."

"I'd suggest that you only visited Pine Gap as a ruse to come here," Brett responded sharply.

The American scanned the room. His eyes locked onto Josh.

"Well, my boss, Fiona Shear, called ahead."

"She was very cryptic in her phone call. So, let's cut to the chase. Why are you here?"

"First, how about I introduce myself to the room?"

Brett grunted.

"I am Lieutenant Commander Patrick Leeson, Navy SEAL. Further to this, I am also a special member of the United States Supernatural Occurrence Taskforce. The American equivalent of your AST. We call ourselves USSOT."

Josh felt a knot form in his stomach. There was only one reason this soldier was here; he knew about the curse. But how could that be?

"So, why are you here?" Liam asked.

"Word has reached US intelligence about your captured lycanthrope. A truly remarkable feat, might I add," Leeson said, sounding genuinely impressed.

Brett and Liam exchanged a look.

"I suspected as much," Brett muttered. "We have a leak in the system."

"Don't be concerned," Leeson started. "I have no interest in requesting data around the lycanthrope. I know our mutual co-operation agreements don't apply in this area. I have something far more exciting in mind."

"Do tell," Brett said, sounding already dismissive towards whatever was coming.

Whether or not the Navy SEAL picked up on his tone, he didn't let it show. "I assume this is our werewolf right here," Leeson stated, pointing at Josh.

Josh said nothing. It was painfully apparent that he was the odd one out in the room.

"Yep, that's him," Brett nodded. Josh admired that Brett always cut to the chase, he wasn't the type of man to ever beat around the bush.

Leeson walked over and shook Josh's hand. "Nice to meet you."

"Ah, yeah, nice to meet you too," Josh said awkwardly.

Leeson turned towards Brett and stated, "We need him for a mission."

Josh's jaw dropped.

"I doubt that is going to happen," Brett peered intensely at the Navy SEAL.

"Fiona Shear will make contact with you, should you agree. She is looking to make a deal between the US Government and the Australian Government for a shared information network. Specifically, in regards to matters of the paranormal. We both know occurrences are increasing. From what our intelligence indicates, you've had multiple lycanthrope appearances in the last year. I know the AST doesn't have the manpower or resources to investigate properly, so we are here to help."

"And you are authorised to speak for your boss?" Brett asked.

"For now, yes."

"Liam, get Josh out of here. I would like to speak with Lieutenant Commander Leeson in private."

Liam nodded and rose to his feet. Josh did the same. As he turned to walk out the door, Josh just couldn't help himself.

"What is the mission?" Josh blurted out.

"We need a monster to fight a monster," Leeson grinned. He winked, and Josh was pulled out of the room.

• • • • •

JOSH SPENT THE NEXT HOUR pacing the length of his quarters. A mission? Did he actually have a shot at getting out of here? The full moon was approaching... there was no way they'd let him go. Or would they? What monster required a werewolf to fight it? Did they need him in human form, or were they going to let the beast loose?

He was desperate for information and now more than ever he wished he had someone to talk to. This was way too exciting to keep bottled up inside.

Josh had actually been allowed, just once, to speak with his parents, Gary and Heidi. They'd been flown to Down Under to be briefed and asked to sign forms swearing them to secrecy. He'd been overjoyed to see them. If the pair of them hadn't fought a werewolf themselves only months beforehand, they would've never believed what was happening to Josh. Gary and Heidi were told in no uncertain terms that Josh's two brothers, Kane and Randall, were not allowed to know the truth. Josh often wondered where they were in their lives. He hoped his whole family were making the most of their freedom.

A knock finally rang out on the door, ripping Josh away from his thoughts of family and the past. The present was calling, and he hoped it was bringing news of escape from sterile white halls.

Brett Sayer stood in the doorway, his eyes piercing Josh.

"Mr Dare," he started, "have you ever been to the USA?"

"No," Josh stated.

"Well, congratulations. You are going."

This was a turn of events Josh had not suspected.

CHAPTER FOUR

THE SURVIVOR

What had transpired in that meeting between Brett and the Navy SEAL, Josh couldn't even begin to guess. Somehow, despite all logic and reason, he'd been allowed to board a military aircraft (under the watchful eye of half a dozen US soldiers) and travel.

No one had given him any specifics about what he was meant to be doing, as was the norm. All he knew was that the United States of America was his destination.

Travelling with Josh was Patrick Leeson, the soldier who'd visited Down Under. Josh quickly picked up on an oddity about the man. Almost every military person they encountered called Leeson, 'Neanderthal'. So much so that Josh started referring to him as that in his head. The guy didn't look remotely like the stereotypical Neanderthal. Josh wanted to ask the story behind the nickname, but thought it best to keep his mouth shut, lest they turn the plane around.

Josh could see that Neanderthal was well-respected among his contemporaries. He was perfectly pleasant to speak with as there wasn't a hint of pride or arrogance in the man. He seemed utterly unperturbed that Josh was a werewolf, almost as if such a thing was a day-to-day occurrence for him. Neanderthal did make a point to mention that Josh's affliction was classified, even among the other USSOT members, and that he shouldn't mention it or draw attention to himself.

Josh was amazed at how absorbed by the scenery he was. Months of staring at sterile white walls had been slowly driving him mad. And just seeing ordinary people again made him feel like he'd lost a piece of himself in his confinement. He wasn't placed in hand-cuffs or discreetly smuggled in and out of airports. He walked among the soldiers like an ordinary man. Josh knew that no matter how fast or strong he was, that he'd never out run a bullet. The Americans obviously knew this too, and for the moment at least, were content that Josh wasn't going to try make a break for it. The thought did cross his mind, but as more of an absurd joke than a real plan. The monster inside of him had killed people, and Josh carried the full weight of that guilt. Part of him felt that he deserved the restricted life he now lead.

The series of flights to get from Alice Springs to the United States were completely uneventful, yet dreadfully tedious.

After a couple of days travelling, Josh found himself in rural

Minnesota.

The countryside was beautiful, and vastly different to Central Australia. There were serene lakes and fairytale forests no matter which direction he looked. He even saw a bear in the wild, which he thought was awesome. It instantly made him consider whether there were other 'were-monsters' out there. Werebears, perhaps? He grinned as he considered the possibility.

The US Humvee Josh now travelled in looked vastly out of place in the remote greenery. Sitting in the back, finally feeling far enough away from Down Under to speak freely, Josh summoned the courage to ask Neanderthal what was going on.

"So, now that we are here… can I ask why?" Josh asked.

"I'm surprised you hadn't asked earlier," Neanderthal answered casually. "You have been very quiet."

"I didn't want to make a fuss…." Josh replied lamely.

"You will receive a briefing when we arrive at our forward operating base. The annotated version is this: USSOT has identified a paranormal phenomenon out here that we don't quite know how to get rid of."

"What kind of creature is it?"

"A wendigo from Native American folklore."

"What is a wendigo?" Josh asked. He felt like he'd read the name somewhere before.

"Basically, endless hunger. A wendigo is a spirit that embodies a craving for flesh. It afflicts those who encounter it with a desire to eat people. It does have other abilities, but that is the part that's concerning to us."

"Cool," Josh said, without thinking.

Neanderthal chuckled and said, "If you saw the bodies, you wouldn't think it was cool. There is actually a medical condition named after the wendigo. 'Wendigo Psychosis' is used to diagnose those with sudden on-set cannibalism."

"What does it look like?"

"By all reports, a wendigo is a giant figure. It was described to me as a bipedal zombie deer."

The image that appeared in Josh's head wasn't comforting.

"And you know that these things are real? They aren't just mythological?"

"They are as real as the werewolf curse. Unlike in Australia, USSOT has a plethora of data from first-hand experiences to draw from. Wendigos have been encountered before. They seem to be intelligent, usually only inflicting their madness on a single passerby before vanishing. However, something is different with this one. For some reason, it is lingering in the forest. There have been multiple victims."

"Why?"

"We don't know. My guess is that something else must be going on in that forest… something we aren't aware of just yet."

"And how do we beat it?"

"We don't know," Neanderthal scratched his chin. "Hence why you are here."

The convoy of military vehicles pulled onto a dirt path and began winding through the tall thin trees of the Pine Island State Forest. They were going off-road.

Before long, they came to a clearing packed to the brim with large tents and vehicles. It looked like an operating centre for at least a dozen people. Everyone was wearing thick boots covered in muck and grime.

"Pine Island Forest is named for the literal islands of pine in a sea of bogs and mud," Neanderthal explained. "Beautiful hiking trails in the area, though."

"Unless being attacked by a monster," Josh interjected.

"That is the exception, not the rule," Neanderthal said. "I am going to speak to the director. You are a flight risk, so armed guards will be with you at all times; however, feel free to wander about."

After being cooped up in the dusty, fluorescently lit walls of Down Under for so long, Josh wouldn't have minded a forest walk. Again though, the thought of being shot for attempting to escape put him off the idea.

He studied the ring of tents. The nearest was long, rectangular and white, with an ambulance parked out front.

Josh walked inside and hit an invisible wall of putrid stench. He soon determined its source.

Right in the middle was a make-shift operating table with a body on it. The dead person was a girl who looked like she'd been clumsily torn apart. Terror was still etched on her face. Her stomach had been ripped open, and she was missing several limbs and appendages. The fate that had befallen her seemed particularly cruel.

A scientist looked up from her pile of notes and greeted Josh. She noticed his discomfort right away.

"New member of USSOT?" she asked casually.

"You could say that…." Josh replied, glancing at the soldiers who'd followed him in. "What is this?"

"Oh, nice accent!" the scientist exclaimed. "You are the Australian, we were told you were coming!"

Josh just stared at the body.

"Only found her last night; she lasted a while in the woods."

"She's a victim of this wendigo?" Josh asked.

"Perhaps... or she is a victim of her friends who fell under the spell of the monster."

"Are they still out there?"

"No, they've all been found. Terrible thing... and those campers aren't the first group this has happened to out here."

"Has anyone survived?"

"Yes, one young man from this camping trip is the sole survivor. I do believe you have been scheduled to talk to him. I can take you now if you'd like?"

Josh shrugged. He didn't know what he was supposed to be doing. This scientist was certainly much more aware of his purpose than he was.

"Come, I'll take you to meet him."

The scientist led Josh out of the medical tent towards a demountable that was partially obscured by the forest. Its door was propped open. As Josh ascended the steps inside, he concluded that this was a holding cell. Iron bars cut off the last third of the structure. Behind the bars was a man sitting cross-legged on the floor.

The prisoner had a wild, deranged look about him. His skin was dirty and his hair was laden with sticks and grass. He twitched nervously as they approached.

"We found him wandering the woods alone. He is in here because we believe he could be a danger to others. Whatever happened out there seems to have dramatically affected his mind," the scientist shook her head sadly.

Josh approached the bars. He empathised with the prisoner. He too knew what it was like to experience the supernatural, then be held against your will.

Josh crouched down and asked, "What is your name?"

The man didn't answer; he just fidgeted slightly.

"Sam Oswald, according to his license," the scientist answered from behind Josh.

"*Screw it,*" Josh thought. "*I might as well try and connect with him, as we are both victims of the paranormal.*"

"I know what it's like, the situation you are in, Sam," Josh said softly.

Sam looked at him curiously. "You've known the madness that crawls from the voids beyond our understanding?"

"What?" Josh said, taken aback. "I mean the supernatural force in the woods."

"Earthly problems," Sam muttered.

It was then that Josh noticed Sam fidgeting with a bizarre-looking pendant around his neck. It looked like a bunch of green tentacles cut with angular lines.

"His mind seems almost gone," the scientist stated.

"Sam, focus," Josh commanded.

An idea came to him. What if he could show the madman his own curse? Back at Down Under, Josh had been experimenting with the power of the dormant wolf during his meditation sessions. He'd found he could search within himself for the curse. It caused a sudden spike of rage and mindlessness to wash over him while increasing his strength for a short time.

Josh sat down on the floor and closed his eyes. He breathed in deep. The full moon flashed across his brain and he followed the white light. The howling of the wolf rang in his ears.

Josh opened his eyes, and they flashed orange for the briefest moment. Anger coursed through him. Josh regained his composure and quickly released his grip on the curse. Almost instantly, he calmed down.

Sam was watching Josh intently. He'd seen the temporary change.

"You are touched by forces beyond the natural order," he murmured, shuffling forward.

"As are you," Josh responded, rubbing his eyes. He felt dizzy.

"My father read the dread book. He danced around the fire while the green idol watched. Now I wait for the slumbering to end and the sunken to rise."

"Enough of that cryptic nonsense," Josh stated abruptly. "What happened in the wood?"

"It hides in the mist," Sam snarled, his teeth bared. "It is not bound to this world. A creature of bone and rotting flesh stalking the woods. It can appear anywhere. Its hunger becomes your hunger. Your thoughts are replaced with its thoughts... to eat... to devour."

"How do you know this?"

"I saw it... it blocked my way to the cabin...."

"How did you escape?" Josh asked.

"I serve a different power now," Sam smiled maliciously. "The beast dares not cross the chaos who crawls. I sought the lonely cabin for answers… answers it seems will be forever denied me. These woods are home to many things."

Josh stood up.

"Have you found this isolated cabin in the woods that he keeps mentioning?" he asked the scientist.

"This is the first I've heard of it," she replied, evidently impressed. "We have found the campsite; it must be near there."

"I guess that is where we need to go. Sam said that the wendigo gets into people's minds? Is that right?"

"As far as we know. Look at Sam. He seems insane, and he survived."

Josh was beginning to understand why he was here. Part of the werewolf curse was madness during the full moon. The madness wasn't part of Zeus's original curse. It came from the Moon Goddess Selene, who had been spurned on the full moon by an ancient Greek king. There was no way the wendigo could influence the werewolf's mind on the full moon, as it was already affected by a goddess.

"Thank you, Sam," Josh nodded, before standing up. Clearly whatever was happening in the mysterious cabin Sam wanted to find was causing the unusual behaviour of the wendigo. Or so Josh assumed.

Josh walked out of the demountable, only to be met again by his two miserable-looking guards.

He avoided going back through the medical tent, instead walking around until he returned to the Humvee he'd arrived in.

The clearing was now occupied by a forklift backing through the leaves carrying a heavy load of boxes.

Neanderthal approached.

"Have you sent any men into the forest to hunt down the wendigo?" Josh asked.

"Yes," Neanderthal replied simply.

"And what happened to them?"

"Unpleasant things. Their minds are broken."

"So, you need an impervious mind to hunt it down?"

"It is a gamble, but a calculated one. Sometimes supernatural beings, just by their nature, can kill other supernatural beings. If it can't get in the werewolf's head, you stand a fighting chance. And tonight is the full moon."

From not far away, the forklift driver swore. He'd attempted to pick up another pallet but had accidentally sent the blade straight through the side of the cardboard boxes on top.

The forklift tore through several layers and a tumbling mess of small silver cylinders fell to the forest floor.

"Silver bullets?" Josh asked.

"Yes," Neanderthal replied. "We may not know how to deal with the wendigo, but we know how to deal with you."

Josh gulped. Whether by wendigo or silver, he hoped this full moon would not be his last.

Chapter Five

THE LONELY CABIN

- JUNE 19 2020 -
PINE ISLAND STATE FOREST, NORTHERN MINNESOTA

Neanderthal had a plan. To Josh, it seemed a little haphazardly made, but he wasn't in a position to question it. The scientists at the outpost had made it clear that the full moon would rise early tonight. Neanderthal was operating under the full assumption that the wendigo would appear once they ventured deep enough into the forest. Under the supervision of a team of USSOT soldiers, they were going to somehow pit Josh against the wendigo.

They now had a secondary objective too. The US team were very interested in the cabin Sam had mentioned. Neanderthal didn't hide his suspicion that something supernatural was happening at the cabin, and that everyone had to be on high alert, as it was an unknown threat.

Neanderthal ensured that six of his men were fully equipped with silver bullets and silver body armour beneath their military webbings. Neanderthal explained that it was an educated guess that silver might hurt the wendigo, but it was mostly just in case things got out of hand with Josh.

Neanderthal was also banking on the werewolf proving to be enough of a foe that it could damage the wendigo. At least enough for it to be taken down with silver bullets. Josh had to bite his tongue not to mention the amount of guesswork that was involved.

The thought of the moon weighed heavily on Josh's mind. There were a lot of innocent people here, and it seemed the Americans were underestimating just how deadly the werewolf within him was. Still, his pending transformation didn't appear to be a big deal to anyone else.

Neanderthal, Josh and the US soldiers, with fully-loaded backpacks, piled into two military vehicles. They began down the remote track to the campsite. That was to be their starting point.

It took a good hour of travelling, and the drivers had to navigate through treacherous bogs and around sinkholes. After getting as close as they could by car, they began walking.

The forest couldn't have been more peaceful. Birds chirped and the wind whistled playfully through the vegetation. The sun was warm and the trees reached high to soak in its solar blessing. Herds of deer ambled through the undergrowth, scattering away as the team passed by. This wasn't a place of supernatural terrors and horrors of the flesh. The beauty of the world was on full display. Josh couldn't think of a less spooky place for a cannibal monster to hide.

When they arrived at the campsite, that all changed. It was clear that the place had already been visited and studied. Tables sat between the tents laden with lab equipment. Or at least they had been. Josh was horrified to see a metal bench completely ripped in half. Shattered glass beakers were strewn around the ground along with hastily discarded notebooks.

The original camp was also a mess. The air was filled with the stink of rotting food. Tents had been torn opened and blood still stained some of the nearby trees. Despite the day being completely clear, small pockets of mist were appearing as the soldiers surveyed the scene.

"The wendigo appeared here," Neanderthal announced, sweeping away some leaves with his boots. "One of the campers ran off down that way, where she rendezvoused with a couple of others. The wendigo followed and inflicted its madness upon them."

"So, we are going that way?" Josh guessed.

"Correct," Neanderthal affirmed. "It seems the further west you go, into the thickness of the forest, the more agitated the wendigo becomes. Perhaps that is the location of this mysterious cabin?"

He signalled to his men to move out.

Josh did feel an ominous vibe in the air. It might have been his imagination, but he felt like they were being watched. As the mist grew thicker, so did his unease.

The soldiers trudged away from the camp, with Josh squarely

in the middle of the group.

After forty minutes of scenic walking and one unfortunate collapse into a bog, they stopped. The forest had undertaken a primeval transformation. Wild trees and untamed life created the feeling they were trudging through the echo of forgotten age. Unseen things flitted about in the mist, causing even the hardened soldiers to get a bit jumpy.

"Satellite imagery doesn't show anything out this way," Neanderthal muttered, swiping across different screens on a tablet.

Josh swiped at a particularly annoying mosquito and missed. It landed on the shoulder of the man in front, who Josh noticed was fidgeting and sweating profusely.

"Hey, are you okay?" Josh asked, tapping him on the shoulder.

"Yeah," he said in a thick southern accent, "just hate the damn the woods."

Neanderthal turned around and closely observed the man. "Sit down," he commanded. "We will have a break."

The hairs on the back of Josh's neck stood up. There was a presence drawing close. The dark shadows of the trees suddenly became threatening as they fell across the group, like they were stuck in a claustrophobic web of nature. The air became thick and heavy and Josh sensed shifting hidden creatures all around him.

Just then, the soldier at the rear shouted in alarm and pointed off into the distance.

The others followed his line of sight. All Josh could see was a large pocket of mist gliding by. There was something else though… something he could smell.

"Do you guys smell that?" Josh asked.

They all shook their heads. "Smells like the woods to me."

"I smell rotting flesh," Josh said slowly. The werewolf curse had left his senses far more attuned than that of the average person. The creature was getting closer and closer, bringing its wretched odour with it.

Neanderthal walked up to Josh and asked, "Do you see anything?"

"No, but-"

A scream echoed out, followed by erratic gunfire. The soldier who'd been looking ill now had his teeth firmly pressed into his comrade's neck. Blood was pooling around the vicious bite.

The other soldiers ran up and wrestled him away with some difficulty.

Josh gasped when he saw the ill man's face. His skin had gone deathly pale and his eyes were pitch black. He looked monstrous.

Neanderthal pulled a medical pack from his military webbing and began closing up the wound on the other soldier's neck.

"Dawson! DAWSON! The hell is wrong with you, man?"

The soldier, Dawson, was writhing on the ground so violently he was proving difficult to keep down.

"Dude, is he trying to bite me?" one of the soldiers asked as Dawson snapped at him.

"Looks like it. You got zip-tie cuffs?"

"On the back of my belt. Roll him over and I'll put them on."

Josh knelt down and assisted the soldiers in securing their afflicted brother. They put the cuffs on, and, for good measure, leashed his legs together with a belt.

From behind them, they heard Neanderthal whisper, "It's here."

Dense patches of mist had formed all around them. The birds had stopped chirping and the trees were still. Not even the wind whispered. Silence hung in the air. The soldiers instinctively held their silver bullet loaded rifles at the ready.

The attack came from nowhere.

A gangly grey arm of immense proportion burst forth from the mist and swiped one of the soldiers off his feet with a bone-shattering impact. The soldiers opened fire, but the arm disappeared into ethereal nothingness as quickly as it'd manifested.

The stench of decay was almost overwhelming Josh now. It was nauseating.

Through the corner of his eye Josh noticed a shadow shifting in the mist. The obscured creature was gigantic. Josh could slightly make out its head. It had vast antlers that spread out behind the tree trunks. It also had glowing white eyes…

Those eyes… they bore into Josh's skull. Madness swept over him. In those shining malevolent eyes, he felt the pull of the wendigo's mind. The hunger… the desire for flesh… it washed over him in a tidal wave of singular emotion.

Josh knew what he had to do. Before he lost himself to the wendigo, he had to find the echo of the wolf within him. Like he had done when speaking to Sam Oswald, he found the lurking shadow quickly and saw the full moon rise in the forefront of his mind. Anger filled his every pore. The madness of the goddess jostled with the hunger of the wendigo.

The blackness couldn't take Josh, and his eyes remained his own.

A shrill hooting sound bellowed out. The wendigo had failed to turn Josh and was voicing its displeasure.

The shadow was all around. In the mist, antlered shapes were flicking in and out of existence. The soldiers shot into the forest wildly, but their guns had no effect.

Neanderthal skillfully dodged a sweeping grey arm and stuck his silver knife into it. Pungent, coagulated blood splattered across him. The wendigo screamed and recoiled. When the arm vanished, the knife fell to the forest floor.

"It is a creature of illusion," Josh thought. *"We need a way to reveal its true form."*

The shrill hooting grew louder and a blinding torrent of mist overwhelmed them. It was so dense that Josh couldn't see anyone else. He breathed in deep and regained his composure. If he stayed too long with the echo of the wolf, there was a risk he could lose himself entirely.

The monstrous shadow loomed behind him. Even though Josh could sense it, he was still too slow.

He was hit in the stomach by one of the mishappen hands and sent careening through the fog. He slammed into a nearby tree with devastating force. He felt his shoulder dislocate, then immediately right itself, as his werewolf healing factor kicked in. It didn't stop him from being severely winded, though.

He heard the soldiers screaming and the shouts of Neanderthal to close their eyes.

Josh got to his feet and moved. The fog was so thick he could barely see a few feet ahead.

He allowed his nose to lead him away from the scent of decaying meat. He wanted to get out of the fog and re-evaluate the situation. The wendigo was impossible for him to fight as he was now.

Then there was the cabin and its mysteries. What if, right now, something was happening nearby that had caused the wendigo to go into a fit of rage and attack. He must be close to the cabin. If he could get there, there was a chance for Neanderthal and his team to be saved.

Josh pushed through the vegetation until he came to the edge of a clearing, and was met by a most peculiar sight.

A strangely designed wooden building sat in the middle of an open space. The area surrounding it was all stinking bog and gnarled trees. Trees so twisted only an unearthly force could have shaped them.

The cabin itself had a high triangular roof and stood on supports that held it out of the muck. There was an orange glow coming from a window built into its almost vertical side. The structure looked like an upright triangular prism.

Resolute, Josh carefully navigated the clearing, being sure to avoid all patches of quicksand.

He came to the door and pulled it open.

Josh was almost crash-tackled by a stranger who was waiting for him on the other side. Josh reacted quickly, side-stepping the man and pinning him against the wall, holding him at bay with ease. The cabin's sole occupant was old, though how old, Josh couldn't tell. He had long white hair that was so filthy it had matted into dreadlocks around his shoulders. His skin was pale and exceedingly wrinkled and he wore a grimy, tattered robe.

The old man screamed gibberish through his missing teeth until Josh put him down.

"Who are you? And why-" Josh demanded.

His question was cut off by a series of chilling sounds. Screams were emanating from several square holes cut into the floor.

Josh rushed over to the nearest one, fearing this man had prisoners trapped here. Roughly a square metre had been cut out of the wood and was left uncovered. Below it was a similarly sized hole in the earth, dug below the cabin's supports. It was too dark to see what was down there. But Josh's attuned senses told him it was something horrible. Judging by the pitch and intensity of the screams, Josh knew it wasn't human.

Noticing Josh's interest, the old man hastily picked up some broad timber cuts and threw them on top of each screaming pit.

It did little to dim the noise. The horrible sounds rose up in a chorus of agony.

"What have you got down there?" Josh demanded.

The hunched old man waved dismissively and muttered, "Things from the abyss... from a dark world." His words were short and broken.

Josh did not feel at ease in the odd home. Scrolls with strange writing and disturbing images were scattered about the floor. Plastic tubs full of a potent-smelling black liquid lined the shelves. In the far corner looked to be a collection of small animal bones.

"Are you some kind of witch?" Josh asked.

"Bah!" the old man shouted.

He fastened his stained-yellow robe around his waist and turned to Josh.

"You, Sam?" he barked.

"Ah, no. I'm Josh."

"Where is Sam?" he cried, his voice raspy and hollow. He didn't sound like he spoke much.

"Sam Oswald? He's gone."

Josh didn't want to tell this nut that Sam was imprisoned nearby.

"Sam said he would come. The time soon approaches; things must be ready."

The entire log cabin seemed to buzz with a strange energy. The air was ominously electric. The screams from the pit didn't let up.

"It is you, right?" Josh said cautiously. "You stirred up the wendigo with whatever you're doing out here?"

"Wendigo… nonsense…" the strange man muttered. He began flipping through a large black book with metal clasps that was propped up on the table.

Josh figured many of the drawings and runes scrawled into the walls could be acting as a ward against the malevolent force of the hunger spirit. The whole cabin had a sinister aura, which felt completely different from that of the wendigo's.

The wailing from the holes continued. Whatever creatures were held down there made anguished noises. Josh had to resist covering his ears to rid himself of the sounds.

"Who are you?" Josh asked.

"No name," he snapped in response.

"Nice to meet you, No Name," Josh replied sarcastically. While the cabin was creepy, Josh was not in any way afraid of the old man.

"Why were you waiting for Sam Oswald?"

"Oswald has been to the library," no name mumbled in his coarse voice. "He has answers. Need to study the missing pages."

Josh noticed that the tattered black book he was reading seemed to be incomplete. There were damaged and torn pages all through it.

"What about his friends?"

"His friends too. He wanted me to show them. I will show them."

"Show them what?"

No Name said nothing.

"Well, all of his friends are dead. The wendigo got them."

Josh's eyes darted towards the grotesque idol by the door. It depicted a humanoid creature with a squashed octopus head on a body wrapped in bat-like wings. It was hideous. It was alien.

No Name noticed Josh staring and said, "The time is soon upon us. In my dreams, I have walked outside this world, and I have seen it. Chaos beckons. The demon sultan gnaws hungrily and perpetually…."

"So, Sam brought all his friends out here to meet you?"

Josh noticed amongst the myriad of papers were typed letters. He picked one up. At the bottom, it was signed Sam Oswald. There were dozens and dozens of them. Sam and this person had been corresponding for some time. Although how exactly this man collected mail remained a total mystery.

"I will show you," No Name sneered.

The old man pointed his finger to the book and started speaking in a dreadful foreign tongue.

"Y'ai'ng'gnah! Yog-Sothoth. H'ee-l'geb. F'ai throdog. UAAAH!"

The words were terrible. The cabin shook on its foundations. The melodious chanting continued on and on as he repeated those demonic phrases. The air in the cabin began to ripple with violent energy. No wonder the wendigo was upset. Josh could feel the old man's chants in his soul.

A colossal crashing sound boomed in from outside. Josh raced to the nearest window of the pointed cabin and saw trees being thrown about. Roots, trunks and all were being tossed into the air like they were the most meager sticks. But, more than this, he could clearly see what was throwing them. Across the clearing was the back of some towering rotten creature.

It was squealing in rage, making its strange hooting sound. Between the tall pines, Josh could see its long, ghastly antlers. The old man's chanting was enraging it.

Despite its evident anger, the wendigo stayed well clear of the cabin. He could hear the desperate shooting of the soldiers in the wood. The wendigo was flailing wildly and Josh feared it could bring down a tree and kill the Americans.

"STOP!" Josh cried to No Name.

"YOG-SOTHOTH-"

"STOP!" Josh yelled again, his hands pressed firmly against his ears.

The purple of twilight filtered into the cabin.

Night was here.

Neanderthal said it would be an early moon tonight too.

As if on cue, Josh's mind went blank. His body started contorting and twisting as he collapsed to the floor.

Amongst the screams of the wendigo and the chanting of the strange man, the werewolf was born again.

CHAPTER SIX

WENDIGO VERSUS WEREWOLF

- JUNE 19 2020 -
PINE ISLAND STATE FOREST, NORTHERN MINNESOTA

The chanting stopped. No Name looked at Josh with a mix of revulsion, horror and confusion. With time had come acclimatisation to the transformation. In less than a minute, Joshua Dare was lost to a muscular mound of midnight black fur, razor-sharp teeth and deadly dagger-like claws.

The last rays of orange from the brief sunset were quickly obscured by the high trees and their long twisted shadows.

Rising behind the triangular cabin was an enormous moon. It was so vast and bright that lunar light blanketed the clearing and filtered into the building, soaking into the werewolf's every pore. In this foreboding twilight the monster was at last unshackled and free.

The occult stranger backed into the far corner of the room as the werewolf rose on its hind legs. It howled, sending its cold terrifying call bouncing off the walls and out into the forest.

At around eight feet tall, its snout, eyes, chest and stomach were distinguishably different from the rest of it, comprising of patches of short grey hairs instead of the shaggy black. This gave the creature an incomplete look.

The werewolf's jaw quivered as it turned to the cowering old man. Saliva dripped slowly to the floor in slow globs.

The cultist's eyes were wide with fear. He backed into a corner, hunched and frail. Frantically, he began muttering something, in a last-ditch attempt to summon whatever horrible power he'd been channelling in the dark woods. It was to no avail. Before he could complete a syllable, the werewolf was on top of him.

For many full moons, the beast had simply watched as people prodded and tied it down. It had desperately wanted to attack. It wanted to hunt. The men in white coats with their needles could've been a tantalising feast had the werewolf been able to get to them.

Finally, it had a victim.

The old man barely made a sound as long teeth sliced through his flesh and organs. Blood poured like red rain as the werewolf thrashed him back and forth.

The monster dropped the occult man, and he hit the floor with a thud. The werewolf let out a victorious howl; a howl which was met with a bellowing from outside. It was the shrill hooting of the mist-bound wendigo.

The werewolf's head snapped to the sound. Its ears pricked up. Something of significant magnitude was moving through the forest towards the cabin.

The werewolf barreled through the door to meet this new supernatural foe.

• • • • •

NEANDERTHAL RACED IN THE DIRECTION of the cabin with his four uninjured men. The fighting had been intense. Luckily, discipline and training had prevailed. No one had shot each other in the chaos of the fog and they'd all managed to avoid the wendigo's gaze.

The full moon was rising high before them. The shrill hoots and growls, sounds of warning, were growing louder. They pelted across the muddy ground and cracked through branches as they followed the noises of the coming battle.

During the wendigo's attack, the silver bullets had been useless as they couldn't hit the damn thing. The creature was a master of illusions that wielded the mist as a mighty shield to hide behind.

Neanderthal's main hope was that the werewolf could force the wendigo to reveal itself. He knew he was grasping at straws, but the rules were vague at best when dealing with the supernatural. His plan to deal with Josh had primarily involved keeping him well supervised up until the point of transformation. Now, the Australian was gone, and the moon in the sky… He now had a loose werewolf to worry about. If it came for them, its attacks would be swift and could come from anywhere…

The soldiers hit the edge of the clearing, causing a flock of startled birds to rise from the tree line and soar across the face of the rising moon.

"Halt," Neanderthal ordered. He could see the cabin, and he could see what Josh had become.

The soldiers crouched, watching as the werewolf moved hesitantly across the clearing.

It sniffed the air cautiously.

"That thing is scary," one of the soldiers murmured. The rest nodded in agreement.

From out the trees came the wendigo. For the first time, they saw the creature's horrific visage plainly.

At two stories tall, the wendigo was as giant as it was hideous. It stood upright on two cloven hind legs coated with thin matted fur. The internal workings of its stomach were wholly exposed. Where skin should be, instead sat organs and intestines pulsing. It looked like the monster had been ripped open, with the missing outer layers of skin extending up towards its neck. The white bones of its protruding and visible rib cage glinted in the moonlight.

Around the wendigo's collarbone, its disgusting globs of brown fur resprouted. Its arms were inappropriately long, at least twice the length of its body, and ended in flat three-fingered hands. Only the elbows had hair. The forearms and upper arms were comprised of sickly grey skin.

The most fearsome aspect of the monster was its face. It had the head of a stag with blind milky-white eyes. It bled from wounds below its jaw, which was torn open, exposing the bones and tendons of its mouth. The wendigo's snarl displayed its pointed fangs. Blood dripped down in coagulated lumps, further matting the fur of its deer legs. Light patches of mist seemed to manifest from nothing and hover around the creature.

There was a silent pause in the clearing. The two monsters sized each other up.

"Look at this," Neanderthal murmured to his team. "We were right. They are going to fight."

Despite the wendigo's obvious size advantage, the werewolf struck first.

It braced, then pounced. Soaring through the air, the werewolf landed on the wendigo's exposed rib cage, digging its claws deep into the monster's organs. The wendigo bleated in pain as the werewolf went for its jugular.

The wolf-man bore down around the wendigo's neck. The wendigo simply vanished with a spray of mist and appeared at the other end of the field. Its blank eyes showed no emotion, yet evil radiated from them.

The werewolf charged again. From across the clearing, the wendigo's eyes shone with deathly white light.

"Don't look!" Neanderthal warned, covering his own eyes.

It was the gaze of endless hunger used to drive its victims insane. As predicted, it had no effect on Joshua Dare's werewolf.

The werewolf ran toward the wendigo, circling around its legs and swiping with its claws. Chunks of rotten flesh were ripped clean from the monster's lower torso.

The wendigo stamped its feet, but the werewolf was too

fast. Instead of further fruitlessly swatting at its attacker, the wendigo summoned circular rings of fog before it. It thrust its elongated arms into them. The rings acted as portals, summoning the arms from thin air to grab at the werewolf. The werewolf yelped as sickly rotten hands wrapped around it.

The wendigo hooted joyously as it attempted to crush the werewolf. The werewolf rallied, calling on breathless strength from within and biting down on the engorged, rotten finger of the wendigo. The wendigo released with a booming cry as the werewolf tore free another long strip of flesh.

Neanderthal noticed the wendigo didn't seem to be healing after the attacks. His initial thoughts might have been correct! Because the werewolf was also a supernatural monster, it could hurt the haunter of the forest.

The wendigo vanished into mist again and reappeared to launch new attacks, seeming more and more unsteady as it did so. The sounds it made chilled the soldiers to the core. They were the calls of another world.

Neanderthal was willing to wager that the wendigo was unfocused, not just due to the fight with the werewolf, but also because of its proximity to the cabin. The place had an affect on the monster. He wanted to know how and why.

The wendigo's hoots and bleats became more desperate as it struggled to swat the agile wolf-man darting around its hooves.

To the US soldiers, it looked like a small bird attacking a hawk. There was nothing the bigger creature could do to get rid of the smaller one. After almost being crushed, the werewolf wasn't playing games. It was out to tear its adversary to shreds.

The werewolf clawed its way up the exposed spinal column of the wendigo and clamped down on its right antler. The US team, even at their distance, could hear it start to break. The werewolf reached across the wendigo's head and dug a long claw into its eye.

The wendigo let out a prolonged and mournful cry.

It then exploded in a suffocating sphere of fog. The orb shot out in all directions with the force of a shockwave.

The werewolf was blown through the air before collapsing into the dirt.

The fog dissipated quickly. Where the giant wendigo had stood was now something else. A terrifying man-sized creature had replaced it.

If this was still the wendigo, it had undergone a startling transformation. It had a human-shaped face devoid of any human features. It had sleeker, smaller antlers springing from both sides of its ominous head.

It had two slits for eyes and a circular, gaping mouth filled with pointed teeth. No longer was it made of exposed bone and rotting flesh, instead having wrapped itself in a thick layer of dark leathery skin. Its arms had shrunk to a proportionate length, and its cloven hooves became two-toed webbed feet. It looked fearsome and deadly. It looked demonic.

The transformed wendigo screamed. The shrill, high-pitched noise was a sound of pure loathing and dread. Neanderthal felt a cold sweat start to drip from his forehead. The cry cut into his soul like a hot knife through butter.

The werewolf howled in return, flexing its muscular arms

and pushing its chest forward.

Neanderthal raised his rifle. There was no longer any mist floating around the wendigo. Its ethereal presence was all but gone. The wendigo was now a much more substantial being, and most substantial beings feel the terrible sting of a silver bullet.

Neanderthal exhaled and moved his finger to the trigger. He had a sight picture.

Before he could take the shot, the demonic black creature blasted towards the werewolf with astonishing speed.

It picked up the werewolf and threw it across the field.

The werewolf's bones crunched as it collided with a tree. The wendigo phased out of reality and appeared by the werewolf.

It squealed in excitement as it threw the wolf again, sending it crashing through the roof of the cabin in a cascade of splintering timber.

Following every movement as best he could with his rifle, Neanderthal finally found a clean shot.

He fired.

The silver bullet whizzed through the air and made contact. It flew into the creature's arm and caused it to change focus. The wendigo turned and gazed at the spot the soldiers were crouched. It locked onto Neanderthal, its injured arm hanging limp at its side.

"The silver bullets work!" Weanderthal exclaimed.

It roared again, its horrific circular mouth grotesquely widening.

"Form a perimeter!" Neanderthal yelled, expecting the wendigo to teleport over and start picking them off. The men shuffled together and pointed their rifles outwards around their leader. Neanderthal unleashed a barrage of silver in the direction of the demonic being.

Now aware of this new threat, the wendigo moved at impossible speed to dodge the incoming hail of bullets.

The momentary distraction allowed the werewolf to recover. Annoyed after being thrown around like a ragdoll, the werewolf bolted out of the cabin. It wrapped its long, black arms around the wendigo, catching it entirely by surprise. The werewolf clamped its jaws around the back of the grey creature's neck.

The wendigo turned its head 180 degrees on its shoulders and clamped its own sucking mouth into the werewolf's fur.

Both creatures attacked with all the ferocity and intensity they could muster.

The wendigo was clearly injured. Its movements were slowing, and the two monsters became embroiled in a fight similar to an old-school boxing match.

The werewolf swung with its claws, and the wendigo dodged and struck back. It was still too fast. Blood was flowing from the werewolf's mouth. It was taking too much damage to keep healing. Something more needed to be done.

"What do we do, boss?" one of the soldiers asked, seeing the peril of their situation.

Neanderthal was thinking quickly. There had to be something in the cabin that could hold the beast at bay, or at least distract it. He had to find out what it was.

"Don't follow me," Neanderthal said, sprinting from the tree line toward the shattered wooden structure.

He slid right by the monster battle and dived inside the cabin.

He saw the jars of black goo and strange green idol, now broken on the ground. Then he noticed the sinister black book and was drawn to it.

Foreign and disturbing images plastered its pages. The drawings were of incomprehensible horrors with unknown words beside them. It didn't take him long to deduce that it was most likely the spells in this black book that had disturbed the wendigo so much.

He flicked through the pages. All of it was madness. He didn't know which particular chant or incantation would assist in stopping the wendigo.

"I need something that will disrupt it enough that I can shoot it in the head or the heart," Neanderthal thought. When in doubt, sending silver into one of those two places usually did the job.

"Screw it," Neanderthal murmured, before opening to a random page. He looked at the foreign words and began sounding them out.

"Z'gai, n'gha e'eh," he mumbled.

He heard the shrill hooting pick up from outside.

Growing in confidence, Neanderthal raised his voice.

"Gro n'hai, a'the! Nya-nyarla…" he'd lost his place.

The entire cabin shook.

"Yog! YOG-SOTHOTH!" he shouted, picking a part of the incantation at random to start again.

Neanderthal's eyes grew dim. The entire room seemed to darken. Something twitched in the newly growing shadows. The chorus of shrieks echoing from the holes in the floor grew louder, becoming a deafening cacophony of noise. The unseen abominations in the pit were afraid.

"Hast. U'geh n'hai e'eth! YOG-SOTHOTH!"

Neanderthal suddenly felt seasick. Everything went blurry. From the far corner of the cabin, a thick black tentacle began sliding towards him. There were tentacles everywhere, spouting from the holes in the wall and snaking their way across the room. Neanderthal looked up and saw that the hole in the roof was now occupied by a gelatinous mass of bubbling eyes.

Neanderthal screamed.

Reality returned as quickly as it had vanished.

A black shadow loomed beside him. The wendigo was here.

He could smell its rotten stench and see its sickly grey skin. Its open mouth was coming towards him. He could feel its hot breath against his skin.

This was the end.

As if in slow motion, Joshua Dare's werewolf barreled straight over the top of Neanderthal and cannonballed the wendigo. It couldn't dodge this time.

Without thinking, Neanderthal raised his rifle and fired. He shot two rounds into the creature's head and two into the chest, where he assumed its heart and brain should be.

As the bullets landed, the werewolf closed its jaws around the wendigo's head, just below its antlers, and pulled.

With a gut-wrenching tear, the werewolf removed the wendigo's head from its body.

It shook the head vigorously and tossed it across the room. The antlers stuck into the far wall with a splinter of wood. Then, in a puff of mist, every element of the creature disappeared.

Clearly confused, the werewolf sniffed the air. It turned to Neanderthal and snarled.

The Navy SEAL raised his rifle, pointing it straight at the beast. One shot would kill it.

He hesitated.

The werewolf was bleeding from a series of deep, unhealing wounds. It swayed unsteadily on its feet.

Neanderthal didn't dare flinch. He just watched as the werewolf growled again, then collapsed to the ground. Its eyes swiftly closed. The werewolf was defeated.

Without daring to blink, Neanderthal radioed back to the outpost, "Bring the silver trap, mission complete."

Neanderthal picked up the tattered black book he'd read from and put it under his arm.

"I'm keeping this," he muttered. "There is a mystery here that needs solving."

CHAPTER SEVEN

A NEW ADVENTURE BEGINS

Once again, hooked up to a bunch of beeping machines within the sterile walls of a hospital, Josh found himself waking up completely disoriented. He was dressed in a blue gown and had privacy curtains on every side.

"What happened?" he croaked, rubbing his head. He hated how the full moon always ended in nudity for him. Someone, once again, must've found him and dressed him.

"Oh, you know, epic monster battle," a familiar voice said from behind the curtain.

Neanderthal pulled it aside and sat down on the plastic stool beside Josh's bed.

"You transformed back into yourself at dawn, and we moved

you here for a basic checkup. Welcome to Minneapolis."

"I'm in the city?" Josh asked. "What happened yesterday?"

"The wendigo problem is dealt with. I think, all things considered, it was a great success. Your werewolf body took such a beating in the fight that it basically shut down. You were very easy to manage."

"And the wendigo is dead?"

"Perhaps, we are still monitoring the forest, but I am certain it is gone."

"Good," Josh said simply. "What about the weirdo in the cabin?"

"That will require some investigating," Neanderthal answered, sounding a little concerned. "Through this little incident, we have stumbled onto some darker powers at work. Nothing to worry about now though."

"So, what was going on in the forest?"

"As far as we could tell, whatever the man in the cabin was experimenting on triggered the aggressive response from the wendigo."

Josh sat upright. "The holes in the floor! The cabin had holes in the floor where screaming was coming from! What was down there?"

Neanderthal shook his head, "I heard the screaming too, but when we investigated this morning, there was nothing. Though the walls at the bottom of those pits looked scratched... like they'd been forcibly dragged away. Another mystery."

Josh was disappointed. He really wanted to know what the madman had imprisoned down there.

"What happens now?" Josh asked.

"That is for Brett Sayer and the AST to decide. We will return you to Australia. There is no immediate rush, the full moon is over, and you are no danger to anyone."

"Damn, I'm starving," Josh said suddenly as his stomach rumbled.

Neanderthal pulled a paper bag full of fast food up from beside him and gave it to Josh.

"Cheers, mate," Josh said as he unwrapped a burger.

"USSOT and the AST will be working a bit more closely from now on," Neanderthal said, primarily to himself.

"Good," Josh replied through mouthfuls of junk food. "Beats being stuck at Down Under."

Neanderthal laughed and stood up. He bid Josh farewell and left the room.

Josh couldn't help but notice the Navy SEAL looked more troubled than the casual conversation had implied.

• • • • •

IT WASN'T LONG BEFORE JOSH was once again sleeping through a tedious series of flights on the way back home.

When he, at last, found himself in the familiar confines of Down Under, it was Brett Sayer that greeted him.

"How was our little co-operative exercise with the USA?" he asked.

"Productive," Josh answered. "I'm sure you got a report."

"I did; we can add this wendigo creature to our data banks.

Having the Yanks around for information might not be too bad."

"I doubt you'll have any trouble with a wendigo in Australia."

Brett laughed and said, "That's what we thought about werewolves. However, in your case, Mr Dare, I think we need to think a little beyond Australia. How the US Government found out about you is troubling."

"Huh?" Josh replied.

"There are forces at work that have their eyes on the curse you carry. We don't know who your location has been leaked to exactly, so we are going to have to move you as precautionary measure."

"Oh, good," Josh stated, surprised.

"We've been liaising with our partners in The Old World. I want to put you somewhere you can be managed effectively, but also somewhere we can hide you in plain sight. Not in Australia though…" Brett said.

"Why not?"

"Government support for the coming mission is proving difficult to secure. That is not your concern though, for the moment at least."

"So, where am I going, then?" Josh questioned.

"Have you ever been to Japan?" Brett asked.

Josh raised his eyebrows.

Perhaps another adventure was just around the corner?

Q_& A

WITH THE AUTHOR

Q: WHY WRITE A NOVELETTE?

A: One of my favourite writers, Matthew Reilly, often puts out short stories that expand his universes and add additional content for fans. I wanted to do something similar, but with a stronger emphasis on actually reading the short story to complete the full picture. The Old World Saga isn't just limited to main series books, as sometimes an important story needs to be told that doesn't require a full novel to do so. Thus the novella series was born.

You can skip the Wendigo Incident, but you will miss the introduction of an important character in Neanderthal and our first catch-up with Joshua Dare in a long time. Plus, the events are frequently referenced in *IN THE SHADOW OF THE OLD WORLD* and set a bedrock for things to come in *FALL SILVER ARTEMIS*. While it isn't essential reading, it is a very fun story and hopefully you lost yourself in it!

Q: WHY WAS THE WENDIGO YOUR FOE OF CHOICE?

A: One of my first ideas, right as I approached the end of book one, was that Joshua Dare would face off against other supernatural monsters. The premise of book two was going to be the battle between a werewolf and wendigo, however, the story quickly evolved and the larger plot was introduced in RISE GOLDEN APOLLO.

Even with the change in direction, I couldn't let go of the supernatural face-off idea. It sounded perfect for a short story. The first book had its roots in horror, and there is no more horrific a monster than the wendigo, a monster that causes cannibalism in its victims. It was also a monster with varying descriptions, allowing me to introduce multiple forms and abilities for it. Just to make the fight even more exciting.

The image of the wendigo, a bipedal zombie deer that haunts the woods was just so captivating that it had to be my monster of choice. So, in the answer in short is, I just think wendigos are cool, that's why I picked it! Plus, combining different religions and mythologies is central to the Old World Saga, so pitting a Native American monster against a Greek one was too perfect to skip.

Q: THAT WAS LOVECRAFTIAN, WASN'T IT?

A: This novelette marks the official introduction of the Cthulhu mythos to the Old World Saga. This thread isn't fully pulled until book four – *FALL SILVER ARTEMIS*. But now was the time to slyly introduce the works of HP Lovecraft into my own writing. In my mind, there is very little that differentiates world mythologies from the original works of Lovecraft. For those who aren't familiar with his works, I recommend all the usual classics: At the Mountains of Madness, the Call of Cthulhu and especially The Case of Charles Dexter Ward, where I have found inspiration for some of the elements in this novelette.

The cult of Cthulhu and the elements around it, as written by Lovecraft, will be canon to my story, though edited to fit my own interpretation. For the purists out there, this does not mean a work like the Call of Cthulhu is a canon story to the Old World Saga. Parts of it may very well be interpreted, but only what is presented in the novels going forward will be the official story. Fans of Yog-Sothoth, Nyarlahotep, Cthulhu and Azathot, rejoice – for that pantheon is joining the story very soon. Terrible things lurk in the cosmic voids, let us hope the fighting between Earthly gods and angels doesn't draw their gaze…

TILL NEXT TIME,

JOEL!

JOSH'S STORY CONTINUES IN:

THE OLD WORLD SAGA BOOK THREE:

IN THE SHADOW
OF THE
OLD WORLD

THE OLD WORLD SAGA SO FAR...

BOOK ONE: IN THE SHADOW OF MONSTROUS THINGS

A European holiday takes a sinister turn when Joshua Dare encounters a werewolf. Feeling its bite, Josh escapes, but soon realises that he is now inflicted with an ancient curse. Having to learn how to manage his full moon affliction, Josh is thrust into a world of secret organisations, government operatives and mysterious strangers hunting him. Josh has entered a larger story of gods and monsters, and this is just the beginning...

BOOK TWO: RISE GOLDEN APOLLO

An Australian spy, Melissa Pythia, is searching for a powerful artefact in Rome. More than underworld figures are on her trail as she learns about her connection to a golden sword.

At the same time, in the distant past, the gods of the Underworld are waging war against the angels of Heaven. The surprise attack on the Olympians leaves Apollo lost in time, and only Melissa can bring him back...

Surviving the deadly bite of a werewolf and fearing a life in chains, Jesse Billiau is on the run. His escape goes awry when he is captured by drug-runners and moved to a secretive compound deep in the forest. When the full moon shines the beast within is released, and Jesse becomes a herald of death and destruction. In his moment of utmost despair, the God of Death, Baron Samedi, reveals to Jesse that his suffering is needed for greater events to come.

Fearing an information leak and seeking to bolster their alliance with The Old World, the Australian Government has moved Josh Dare to Japan. He is soon tracked down by malevolent supernatural forces who want to exploit his curse. He is the best link to the empty position of Zeus, the vanished god-king. Now, a small team of Australian and US operatives need to work with the gods of old to fulfill an ancient ritual and stop that power falling into the wrong hands.

Novella Three: EARTH'S MIGHTIEST WARRIOR

Long ago lived a warrior renowned as the greatest to ever live. Sigurd of the Volsung line has had his story told through the ages, though not all of it. It was thought his tale ended with his death, but then came the war of gods and angels. Now, Sigurd survives as a rat and a champion in Lucifer's new Hell. The tale of Earth's mightiest warrior is only half told. The new legend of Sigurd takes him across the fiery planes of the Underworld, with beings far beyond Norse myth, on his greatest adventure yet.

Book Four: FALL SILVER ARTEMIS

Danni Quinn has completed her training and is on her first mission. The goal: finding an artefact of the lost God Zeus. Danni and her boss, the reincarnated Oracle of Delphi, Melissa Pythia, set out to find the Goddess Artemis. Travelling across the scorched plains of Hell they meet the long dead hero, Sigurd the Volsung, who agrees to aide them on their quest. Danni's team heads down a path towards sunken cities and alien horrors. With the help of her former flame, Joshua Dare, and the rest of the AST, Danni will risk everything to complete her mission…

Randall Dare thought he was solving a complex equation. Little did he know that the act of writing some numbers on blackboard would catapult him across dimensions to a strange realm known as the Dark World.

Now, as he works to find a way home, he must face off against the monstrous octopus-headed aliens, cosmic gods and the mysterious creatures that call the bizarre planet home. And time is ticking, as Randall is carrying a warning that needs to reach the team back on Earth. Something dreadful has woken up, and his new allies can help to stop it...

WITH MORE COMING SOON!

www.ingramcontent.com/pod-product-compliance
Lightning Source LLC
Chambersburg PA
CBHW030438120726
47903CB00003B/1019